BACK
Copyright © 2015 Steve Hussy
ISBN: 978-1-326-20933-9

10 9 8 7 6 5 4 3 2 1
First Printing

Cover and Interior Art © 2015 Steve Hussy

For all queries contact:
Murder Slim Press, 29 Alpha Road, Gorleston, Norfolk.
NR31 0LQ   United Kingdom

Murder Slim Press are:
Steve Hussy and Richard White

Published by Murder Slim Press 2015
www.murderslim.com

Printed and bound in the UK by the MPG Books Group,
Bodmin and King's Lynn

For Seymour and Rob

Back

Introduction
by
Seymour Shubin

Steve Hussy was in his twenties when, quite happily, he quit teaching at a college. Put it all behind him. Or so he thought. A few years later, a business associate having screwed him, he applied for a part-time position at the same college, which at one time he'd hoped he would never see again. Perhaps to his surprise, but more likely theirs -- for he had been known to be his own man -- they took him back.

Lucky for them. And lucky for the students who were to come into his life. And, oh yes, lucky for us.

The college got themselves one hell of a teacher. And we have in hand one hell of a writer.

Mr. Hussy, now 34, teaches media and film courses. He helps his students, almost all of whom come from low-income families, make films rather than simply analyze them. And he speaks their "language." For instance he swears, he says, "more than is acceptable." (Readers will vouch for that, but I hope it will be the unusual one who won't accept it as part of a true story.) For instance, in his classroom, "Say what you like about fart and sex jokes. They don't truly demean like sarcasm does. That's why I banned it in my classroom."

Funny, yes. And true.

Mr. Hussy is unsparing in offering his feelings -- mostly dislikes -- of teachers and, indeed, the "system." The only thing wrong with teaching, he maintains, are the teachers.

But he is hardly a misanthrope.

"I learned to love teaching," he says, which is a far cry from that young man who couldn't wait to quit.

Mr. Hussy has plenty to say about the change, which alone would make this story must reading.

I offer a hearty thanks for showing us why.

And for doing it so well -- and entertainingly.

Seymour Shubin
Philadelphia, 2011

--- BACK ---

by Steve Hussy

1

I turn the pages of a book, feel the blank walls around me and enjoy it. This can last for a good hour because the staff/disabled toilet is largely unused. On the rare occasion another teacher has dropped their load, that smell is preferable to hearing the same waste spout from their mouths.

I had to go back. I had been screwed out of thousands by Thomas Salter through buying CDs and records for the Murder Slim shop. Salter delayed opening the shop, month after month, and it transpired he'd been selling stock to friends and spending the money on himself. Salter wanted pear wine to drink and an oily rag to sniff. And, above all, he wanted to look like a hero to his cronies. The guy had always loved to rant about his own magnificence and now he could do so while doling out good, cut-price music.

So I was forced back to work, but this time I had it figured out. Two years of thought had gone in to how to avoid as much

Back

risk as possible. After my previous teaching stint had driven me to near-insanity, this time I'd carefully figured out my rules for institutional survival...

1. Always looks busy and walk quickly. If you see a teacher sidling towards you, wave cheerily and take a different route.
2. If cornered and asked about your life and views, reverse the question and then leave as soon as they've finished yapping.
3. Sit in a toilet during busy staffroom periods. Always check your pigeonhole during the middle of lessons.
4. Never talk during staff meetings unless prompted. If prompted, seem confused yet affable. Never talk too much.
5. Never compromise your teaching style. Students aren't your enemy. If they like you, they're forgiving and accommodating.

That all sounds benign, but I didn't want to raise hell again. As a guy in my twenties, I had exploded during a couple of meetings and been caught drinking booze. I had even called some students a cunt. Rarely – mind you – and they truly deserved it.

But this time I thought I could survive it and remain

unscathed. I had no thought of promotion or a career, much as I didn't want a wife or a family. All I wanted was to teach lessons to the best of my ability, to have a decent amount of quiet each day, and the opportunity to read or watch or write stuff.

Teaching meant I could work the least hours for the most money. And hell, I was older and wiser. Wasn't I?

2

I've been a teacher since I was twenty-one.

I had no job in mind during my schooling, but after filling out a computer survey I'd been given a list of suitable jobs.

The first of those jobs was "secretary."

Well, fuck me.

It reminded me of my terrible social skills. I was lousy at small talk and was often inadvertently offensive. This wasn't a problem when I worked bar for three years. Drunks love a sleazy line. But in a *normal* job?

I considered various jobs which were self-reliant. Writer? I wasn't good enough at that. Journalist? I would have to write about crap. Male prostitute? Too nervous. In its own weird way, teaching was the best fit.

Straight after my English and Film degree ended, I went back to the college I'd attended three years before. In the UK, colleges are for 16-19 year olds, and it'd been the most fun I'd had in education.

I had hated school. Aside from being forced to study Maths and other subjects I had no interest in, the atmosphere is one of impending violence. There were borderline insane teachers... I had a German teacher who would sob loudly in his cupboard after we did badly in a vocabulary quiz. And there were a lot of psychotic students... I had one of those fuckwits knee me in my left eye during a cross country run.

That knee permanently fucked up the vision in the eye but also clonked a little thought into my head. It forced out a little of the sarcastic indifference I'd built up around myself.

College gives you an opportunity to weed out the biggest assholes. It's non-compulsory and you also get to pick the subjects you want to do. You even get a good dose of free time. It's a more relaxed atmosphere and a definite improvement from the dictatorial schools.

The college was much smaller back then... just a few hundred students. Many of the teachers were eccentrics. They were from the days before the National Curriculum, which enforced a fixation on the grades needed to attend university.

My favourite was Mr. Greene, my History teacher. He was an unassuming bearded guy touching sixty who looked after his recently disabled wife. He'd tell us largely untold – yet true – tales. Like how the 1905 Russian Revolution failed because Lenin's train into Moscow was late. Or how Napoleon lost at Waterloo because he had piles and couldn't ride into battle.

Although it seemed at odds with my personality, I gradually learned to love teaching lessons. The same thing had no doubt happened to Mr. Greene too. He was a quiet man with a simple love of history who found his inner storyteller.

My own love remains. I get to rant about a lot of great movies, try out various real-life stories, and help students understand – and hopefully enjoy – worthwhile films.

But I do wonder why I'm here. I fluked into teaching – through various illnesses and the main Media tutor quitting to write Roman mystery novels – and then suddenly *I* was a teacher. Huh? I was comfortably the youngest teacher and was voluntarily thrown into a confusing world that took me years to figure out.

Look, the only real problem with teaching is *teachers*. I've been around them for so many years, it's embarrassing to call myself one of them. I teach but please don't call me a teacher.

3

I come from a working-middle class background. I grew up on a housing estate, but it was a plush one where people mostly owned their own houses. My father was the accountant for a company that supplied arcade games and fruit machines. Before she got sick, my mother was a hairdresser and then a housewife.

I don't talk in a similar way to other teachers. I still have a local accent and I swear more than is acceptable. I also have a base sense of humour. But say what you like about fart and sex jokes, they don't truly demean like sarcasm does. That's why I banned it in my lessons.

Teachers' main strategy to control a class is to be a bigger asshole than the students. They respond to problems through snide insults... always wordplay and sarcasm rather than direct comments:

"Why don't you come up here and teach the lesson? I'm *sure* you could do a better job than me."

"Well, I suppose if you didn't understand *anything* you'd think that might be correct."

A fart joke has no victim. It's a universal problem. And tales of sexual dysfunction put yourself as the butt of the joke. It also shows you can't be shocked or offended, which is the main way students will try to get at you.

My first role was teaching a GCSE Media course to students who'd failed at school. One kid, Jonjo, was now touching 19 (just two years younger than me) and was a hulking 6'4" presence. He happily told me that he was an "internet pioneer." He would video himself and his girlfriend fucking on a webcam, and sell passwords to look at the footage. For a guy who'd failed a lot of courses, the guy certainly knew his way around a computer.

This was in the days before DVDs, and I'd have to laboriously set up video clips the night before. Fast-forwarding and rewinding could take a couple of hours.

Halfway through my twentieth lesson or so – on film noir – I felt a familiar gurgle in my stomach that meant I quickly needed to shit. Irritable bowel syndrome. I was nervous early on, getting over that in-built fear of public speaking.

I made my apologies, squirted in the toilet, then returned. I popped in the next videotape and... oh... A porno of a cock entering an asshole in extreme close-up, a little gob of spit dribbling into the black cave before ol' dick probed in. I had – and still have – an aversion to anal sex, and the whole thing set me back on my heels.

The class erupted into laughter.

Back

"You get yer tapes mixed up?" Jonjo said, and laughed wildly.

It's times like when you live or die. Asshole teachers flip out. Exert power. And by doing so, they signal their prissiness. Respectable folks blush and set themselves up for more pranks.

The trick is to *go further*. You can't do that in school, but you can at college. You can't get fired for cursing. For all their tendency to push boundaries, students have limits too. They can be shocked.

"That's not me," I said. "My cock is way bigger than that in my videos."

I then went on to say how the woman looked bored. I described how to tell if a woman has had an orgasm. The six previously disaffected students were damn interested in that. About the nipples hardening, and the boobs puffing out before sagging at the moment of orgasm.

Hopefully the guys treated their gals a little better after that. Hey, I'm a *public servant*.

"WHAT ARE YOU TALKING ABOUT!? WHAT IS THIS DISGUSTING TALK!?"

I looked over to my left and there – steaming in the doorway – was Mrs. McKay. She was an English Literature teacher from the classroom next-door. A 50-year-old Lutheran married to the Computing teacher.

"WHERE IS YOUR TEACHER!?"

The group laughed again.

"Hello," I smiled at her, "I'm the new teacher."

She looked at me for a good ten seconds.

"I'M REPORTING THIS!" And, with that, she stormed off.

I never copped any flak for it... but I did start to talk more quietly.

I had learnt that teachers are almost exclusively smug, phony left-wing, backstabbing, pseudo-intellectual, frequently stupid, hypocritical cunts.

But I better explain all that.

And why you need to run, fucking run, from them.

4

I had re-applied for the job when my old college advertised it in January. No reply. Three months later another ad reappeared with "previous applicants need not reapply... your application will automatically be considered". So I waited.

Back

Nothing again.

Then, during the summer break, the position came up again. Same post, teaching BTEC Media Studies. BTEC is a more practical version of Media, where you help students make films rather than analyse them. This lets students understand what a hard process filmmaking is, and gain a true appreciation of the form. Plus I could teach how to create low-budget gore effects... and what's more fun than fake-vomiting in front of a class full of kids?

Money was running low and I thought I had little to lose. I wrote an aggressive letter demanding to know what was going on. I argued that they knew I could turn up the next day and teach effective lessons.

The next day I was called in for an interview. By Maury Wilson. The head honcho. A living, breathing Thunderbird puppet.

Wilson had been the principal when I had quit a couple of years before. The guy will still be here aged 100. At the turn of the next ice age, for all I know. The guy looks and acts as if he's preserved in formaldehyde every night. Stained crevasses around the corners of his mouth from a constant, eerie grin.

"Hello there," he said, slowly shifting into the same telegraphed smile I'd grown to hate. Then came the overly strong handshake, and the usual look straight into your eyes.

I met his gaze and smiled back. I'd had a long sleep the night before, and a hefty hit of gin and coke followed by a lot of tooth brushing. I was semi-drunk, but had the minty fresh breath of an innocent.

Here we go, I thought, here we go.

5

Wilson led me up to his office. It was the only place in college where you have to walk up steps. He was in casual, summer clothing.

"I'm sure you're wondering why we've taken so long to get in touch. We were concerned about numbers on the BTEC course."

I plonked down on the seat and my legs scrunched up in front of me.

"It's good to see you again," he said, and smiled again. In a way he'd already won. I was back.

"How have things been?"

I squirmed in my tiny, low seat. I was now looking up at a

guy who was a good six inches shorter than me when we were standing up. It shouldn't be disconcerting, but it is.

I went on about staying in New York and Norway. I cut out anything about the Murder Slim shop and any failures. I said I was doing design work here and there. I was, but I avoided how terribly it paid.

Remember it this time... NEVER TALK TOO MUCH.

Wilson smiled throughout but his eyes were disinterested. I thought of him rutting his Maths' teacher wife with the same dead expression on his face.

Then he flipped into business mode. First a little adjustment of his glasses, then a slight rise in his seat. Movements practiced in business courses, along with those annoying delayed pauses where you're supposed to hang yourself by jabbering on.

"Well, it's been debated a lot behind the scenes."

Lengthy pause. I stayed quiet.

"You have many strengths: your students achieve the highest possible levels, you're an inspirational teacher..."

There was more, but I was tuning out and waiting for the "but."

"But..." There you go. "You can be too controversial and ultimately..." and I never thought I'd actually HEAR these words, "...you're not a team player."

Back

My immediate reaction was to gasp – but I held it in – and then I had to stop myself from laughing. This was writing GOLD... and I made sure to jot down the conversation straight afterwards.

"I've always helped teachers when they've asked for it." My defence mechanism and the booze had kicked in. "And I've never needed to ask anyone for help. I deal with stuff with my students alone. I think that's damn important." I shrugged. "I'm self-sufficient."

He paused for a couple of seconds then locked me with his ol' stare: "Of course," he flashed that eerie smile, "but there's also the general feeling that you teach boys better than girls."

I smiled: "Do you have any statistics on that? My impression was that my students – male and female – got grades well above their other subjects. Amongst the best in the country."

"But it's well known you tend to teach somewhat... masculine... films."

"Horror films are now watched by a roughly 50/50 split of men and women."

"Well..."

"But I guess you raised the same problem with the female teachers all screening romantic comedies and alienating male students?"

Wilson crumbled slightly: "It's only an impression."

Shit, I was winning.

Wilson looked down and put in a couple of seconds' thought. Then he looked up again with a "fuck you" smile: "And how is your alcohol problem?"

I flinched – wondering if he'd noticed a smell of gin. "I never had an alcohol problem."

Another pause, shorter than the last one.

"Well, let's give you the guided tour, old chap."

I stood up awkwardly and stretched my back.

I'd been stupid to think the boozer tag wouldn't be gossiped around until it had become "truth."

6

Despite Wilson saying the BTEC course numbers were the primary reason for the long wait for an interview, I had wondered whether the alcoholic shtick was behind it.

I did – and still do – drink. Much more than is medically ok. But *never* to the point of stupor... no-one has ever seen me shit-faced. I also never drank before – or during – teaching during my first stint at college.

Unfortunately, I'd fucked up a key aspect when it comes to dealing with other teachers.

Never trust them. Never show any side of your personality that can be used as a weapon. This will be used to impress their friends and *especially* to impress their superiors. The huge amount of management posts means that it's an ugly case of survival of the fittest. Well, survival of the most sarcastic and most career driven.

I'd been naïve enough to attend a party a few weeks before I was due to quit. I had already handed in my notice, and my summer birthday meant that it hit on a day when I had the afternoon off. I had trotted down the pub with some friends and the friendliest of my students. At this gathering, my co-editor at Murder Slim Press met his now-partner of six years.

We had a good time, full of the usual round of entertainingly sick stories. The kids were over-18, so we weren't even getting into illegal territory. Yeah, someone projectile vomited. But where's the fun in drinking without a little projectile vomit?

Everything was going fine until the Dance teacher walked past. Harriet was a new teacher, eager to climb up the ladder. She was revered as pretty, but I never understood why. Bland yet cynical attitude, long face and dead eyes that showed much more than the easy smile she liked to flash.

She – badly – acted surprised at us sitting in the bench outside the pub. But I fell for it and waved her over. Looking back, she'd obviously got some tip-off I was there.

"Having a good time?"

"Yep!" People chimed in.

"Come 'ave a drink with us," I said. Fucking idiot.

Harriet didn't drink any booze but watched with interest for an hour, whilst joining in good-humouredly with various conversations. She seemed unconcerned and happy.

I started to think I'd misjudged her. The act was too good to be an act. My students – and even my friends – warmed to her.

She went back to work, and we all went home after a few hours. No harm done, aside from me catching sunburn.

Shit, why was I even quitting teaching? It had been a good day.

Well, the next day wasn't... from the moment I walked into the morning meeting.

Suddenly younger teachers were looking at me. Oddly too... smirking sometimes. Harriet gave me a particularly smug look, and whispered to the Music Technology teacher next to her. They both gave a little laugh. Hmmm...

Back

Meanwhile, a good number of the older teachers were looking at me as if I'd just dumped in their mouths.

I've often wondered why the gossip-mill churns so quickly. The standard answer is that people need excitement in their lives. They find their lives so boring that they seek out shit to spice it up.

But I'd take it further than that. By bitching about other people, they justify themselves. And, like too many professions, teachers soon become competitive. They want promotion. They want to show they are *professional*. They want to bury any outside thoughts that they have. And the best way to define *professionalism* is to decry anything outside of the suit, the tie, and the distance from the students.

Within a week, I was probably not only a drunk but also caught in some gangbang outside of the pub. Eating out a 16 year old while a male student licked my ass and another gal fellated me.

Sure, they'd express it all in prettier ways than that. But gossip is gossip... and there's no smoke without fire, huh?

Back

7

Wilson led me around the college on his tour. A new sports hall. A new science block. Student numbers were now touching 1,700. He didn't say anything else about booze, but I checked my breath a few times to ensure there was no smell.

Wilson offered me the BTEC job and I took it.

I sat on my bed that night and thought about the fact I'd be teaching again in a few days time.

The booze issue reminded me of what I feared after just a year of starting teaching. I may have only been twenty-one, but you have to be pretty dim to not sense when people have a problem with you. I was young, male, white, and apolitical. I had imagined them sniping at me from afar. Perhaps it fed into my supposed hero complex where I was always convinced I was right and different.

As a Film teacher, I had taught films that were deemed *common* by my fellow teachers. *Raiders of the Lost Ark, The Texas Chain-Saw Massacre, Barfly, Dawn of the Dead* and so on. Meanwhile they liked to watch – and teach – dreary social realist films where they could gaze at stereotypes of the working class from a safe distance. Their favourite filmmakers had no directorial chops and precious little ability for realistic dialogue. Mike Leigh. Shane Meadows. Ken Loach. My fellow Film teacher was the worst of these: teaching British social realism, alongside such gems as Iranian cinema, Algerian cinema and fucking *Billy Elliot.*

As a perk of the Film course, you get to see the odd free movie here and there. Local councils run these for students and teachers. One year it was Shane Meadows' *Somers Town.*

At one particularly stupid moment – where a heavily overweight Cockney "Del-Boy" stereotype pulled money from his jockstrap – my fellow Film teacher exploded into laughter.

"HAR-HAR-HAR!"

I sat back in my seat, glad I had found somewhere in the screening room away from other people.

"HAR-HAR-HAR!!!" It was genuine laughter, and some of her students joined in.

But what was she laughing at? Would she laugh at a fat guy pulling money out of his jockstrap in real life? Or would she slap him and be vastly offended?

"What did you think of it...?" she asked me afterwards.

"Not much," I said. "Irritating, really."

She looked stunned and a little sniffy: "But didn't you like the people *clinging onto humanity...* Surviving somehow...?"

Back

This wasn't humanity. This was the middle class view of how the poor live. From the Northern runaway kid eating a Polish sausage and getting diarrhoea. To the Del-Boy character, a shonky salesman of sun-chairs. All of it was in tediously grainy black-and-white. Realism, apparently, doesn't come in colour.

I was starting to twitch with frustration, wanting to explain all of that. But if I launched into some attack, it would travel around college within a day. Every little action is magnified when you don't fit into a group. And my tendency is to say the most inappropriate thing because I'm easily bored and edgy.

I needed to figure out a way to remain unconcerned around other teachers. Booze always calmed me, while I'd learned to stay clear of coffee, cocaine and other stimulants.

Teachers stand around drinking endless cups of coffee, chain-smoking and dribbling over their choice of biscuits. But booze is an absolute no-no.

I resolved that vodka was the way to go. Always before interaction with other teachers. It's largely odourless. Even if I could last just a year, my low overheads would mean I'd clear a thousand quid or so.

But, shit, had I become what they had constructed me to be? An alcoholic?

Focus. Keep to the rules. And do what is needed to keep to

them.

Just make sure to keep brushing those teeth with the strongest toothpaste you can find.

8

Donna was the first kick to the nuts.

Donna was the other BTEC teacher. She was in her early fifties and is amongst the most evil people I've known. Yes, she wasn't a serial killer – I haven't known any of those – but she was another nervous breakdown away from slitting throats. My German teacher at school had sobbed out of despair, while Donna seemed to pour all the near-lunacy inside and into a desire to destroy.

It wasn't hard to see why the bosses were worried about the BTEC course. And the issue probably wasn't with me, but some calculation about whether the course could sustain itself.

Five students were doing the course. FIVE. A standard class is 20 or so, yet this course existed with five. Baffling. A practical and "fun" course, where students got the chance to make movies.

Back

Ah, Donna. Two minutes and you knew she was the reason it was failing.

The kids hated Donna. They'd labelled her a lesbian (she wasn't) and visibly withered when she was around.

Donna had taught the group for a year, reducing the number from 12 to 5. Three girls and two guys.

Jewel: heavily overweight and very smart... had rarely had praise because people fixated on her weight. *Rhoda:* wildly sarcastic and defensive, secretly negative about herself. *Kerry:* very tall, self-consciously ditsy and eager to please. *Gary:* a fostered kid now living alone... intense, quiet, angry. *Jack:* fun-loving guy with ambitions to carve a career spray-painting cars.

They were normal students. Each year is filled with kids like these. Individuals with fuck-ups and upsides. Around 90% of kids can be reached in some small way... if only by saying nice things for the first time, or being the first to challenge their prejudices. Some will hate you, but most want to like their teacher. The *vast* majority are good kids finding their way.

You very seldom truly change kids. Long term, you change one out of twenty. But you change all of them for the time they're in your lesson. This is a tiny part of their lives, so it's important to try and make it memorable.

As much as anything, education gives students a little time

to breathe before a grinding job and a demanding family kick in. You hope to help them think, to see other things... even just for an hour or so.

Above all, you like your students. The job is pointless without liking them, for all their occasional anger or bone-headedness. You like listening about their relationships and their home-lives. As a teacher, you are a paid friend as well as a paid educator. You love seeing any progress, even the briefest glimpse.

Yet Donna didn't like her students. She hated them. And that's not a word I throw around. She wouldn't plan lessons. She'd throw together movie clips minutes before she had to teach. She spent much of her free time bitching about the students. How Rhoda was selfish, Kerry was stupid, Jewel was fat and lazy, Jack was a "chav," and that Gary would kill us all. I even broke a couple of rules and defended them. Her relentless stream of hatred could break through anything.

Donna was the embodiment of the secret thoughts that too many teachers have. An increasing sense of superiority over their students coupled with a simmering dislike of them. A bad lesson is always the students' fault. Bad results are always the exam board's fault. And all that bad stuff can always find a listening board with other teachers bitching about the same thing.

The staff room is the home for it. The older teachers sit on easy-chairs in the middle, drinking coffee and whining about problem students. The younger teachers sit on the two banks of eight computers, drinking lattes and yakking about the same issues as they post Facebook messages.

All of them hopped up on a caffeine fuelled power trip and, in their own way, all desperate to fit in.

9

Look, I will admit – out of that first year of BTEC – Rhoda *could* be hard work. She was sniffy and difficult, with a low attention span.

But that sort of thing should fire you up to speed up your lessons. Lessons need a sense of rhythm. It's easy to accommodate for this when you teach Film. Just make sure to show a movie clip every ten minutes. It gives the students a mental break. And it forces you to split the lesson into paragraphs.

One Wednesday, I'd waffled a bit too much and sensed how boring I'd become. The BTEC course is very work orientated, so I asked them how their jobs were going. Almost all of the BTEC students had part-time jobs, as they all came from low-income homes.

Kerry was cleaning caravans. Jack was living his dream and learning about paint mixtures in a garage. Jewel was a glass collector in a shitty pub. Gary wasn't in work, but as a fostered kid he needed to attend college for 90% of his lessons to receive money from the government.

Rhoda – now alert after she'd been given the chance to talk about her life – was working for a large newsagent.

"How is it?" I asked. "Do you want to do something else?"

"I hate it. It's stupid," she laughed and crossed her eyes. "Stoo-pid!"

"Tell 'im about your boss," Kerry said.

"Is he a scary fucker?" I said.

"Nah, not that. Not really. He's a dick though. All the time..." She thought for a second. "I'll be working, like, in the basement bit. We put stock out there. But I never do it quick enough for him. He likes to shout. I mean he really does!"

"Welcome to the world of bosses."

But Rhoda's eyes then got weirdly dreamy. "But I still love him."

"What?"

Kerry was laughing already, and Rhoda slapped her on the

arm. Gary, Jack and Jewel were quiet but honed in on the conversation.

"I love him. He's well fit."

"What?"

"And he's got a nice car too. He let me sit in it once! It didn't have a roof!" Again, she became lost in thought. "I'd do him." She laughed, and Kerry joined in. "I would!"

Maybe I was tired, but the whole thing annoyed me hugely. I took a few deep breaths, but they didn't help. I tried to structure my response into something that would come across as a joke.

"You know what the problem with the fucking world is?"

No response. The students were suddenly oddly quiet.

"TOO MANY CUNTS FUCKING ASSHOLES!"

This was supposed to be the line that would get the laugh. I smiled to try and help prompt it. But the students – even the upbeat Kerry – just stared forward.

I slowly looked over my right shoulder. There, in the doorway from the computer room, was Donna. Shit. A modern-day Mrs. McKay. A repeating, timeless stereotype. People can't chug smoke out of their ears, but Donna was having a good attempt at trying to.

She harrumphed loudly. "I'll leave you with this

SEXIST." She stormed out. I looked back at the group and met their smiles. Jack's and Gary's were largest, but they'd misinterpreted things.

What I said WASN'T sexist.

It was pointless chasing after Donna and telling her that. You don't change the mind of these people. But I did enjoy telling the group why it wasn't.

I sat down.

"Flip the words around in what I just said. 'Too many assholes fucking cunts.' Donna would STILL find that sexist towards women. Even though you're actually insulting both groups."

Ah, maybe it was too easy to put Donna down. I was feeding into the students' dislike of her. But I never hung out with her and I never pretended to be her friend. And in teaching that's rare. They creep around each other. The fuckers are always trying to work some angle. The holy grail of promotion. The dream of more money, your own office, and LESS teaching.

The older a teacher gets, the less they want to teach.

And the older they get, the more they want to redress injustices that existed 30 years ago... simply feeding into a new wave of pointless injustice.

Back

10

That Donna incident – along with a number of others – confirmed one of the weird biases of college and school teaching.

The profession is now vastly outnumbered by female to male teachers. Out of my bosses, eighty percent are female. Out of the total teachers in college, there is an 75/25 split from female to male.

The prominent shift towards female teachers isn't accidental. Many male teachers are forced out the profession early on, caught in "sex scandals." These are sometimes true, sometimes bogus. But they are always taken with deadly seriousness, and soon are manufactured into truth through the gossip mill.

The interesting thing is I've heard more rumours about female teachers fucking male students. But these are passed off much more easily as male students making up stories. In teaching, the woman is typically cast not only in the role of victim, but also as superior.

It's not hard to figure out where this comes from. After hundreds of years of male domination, feminism has rightly searched for equality. But it's now pushed beyond. Female teachers and students are often laden with a sense of superiority. They have the knowledge they can't be challenged by guys because they can stick the "sexist" tag onto them.

"Teaching horror films again, then...."

"Yep. *Day of the Dead* this year. I fancied a change."

"You do realise they're sexist, don't you?"

"Huh?"

"Even with the *final girl* stereotype, they're just giving male viewers the chance to voyeuristically watch the female heroine suffer."

I shrug. "Horror is forward thinking. That's what I teach my students."

I could name tens of horror films that push against negative stereotypes, but what's the point? Keep to the rules. Choose your battles.

But, fuck, even I can't smile as the other Film teacher says:

"Oh, you're such a *m-a-n*..."

11

Donna lasted for three further years. It did feel like an eternity, but it didn't entirely crush my job.

I liked the vast majority of my students without having to try. And by being a part-time teacher, my interaction with her was limited enough that I still tentatively looked forward to each workday.

I only had to deal with Donna once or twice a month, in tedious meetings about the (now suddenly expanding) BTEC course and to check whether we were marking essays evenly.

There were arguments, of course. Thankfully, even the fuckwit teachers had largely taken a dislike to Donna. Face-to-face they were pleasant to her, but they bitched loudly behind her back.

I avoided any trouble from the couple of outbursts I did have. There was one argument over restructuring the movie trailer unit. I wanted to veer this towards horror, because it's a genre that can have real power even with tiny amounts of money. *Re-Animator, Brain Damage, Combat Shock, Street Trash, Evil Dead.*

Donna wanted them to make Westerns. *Westerns?* There are many great westerns, of course, but how can kids work in that genre with a twenty quid budget? She equated challenging or unpopular genres as good for the kids. I dug my heels him and she dug into a rant at me.

"EVERYTHING HAS TO BE DONE YOUR WAY! THIS IS WHAT THEY NEED TO DO! IT WILL MAKE THEM THINK FOR A CHANGE!"

I shook violently. Outside of college I would have flipped, but I dutifully bit my lip and looked at her. She stormed off again, like the teens she seemed to find so petulant.

Urgh... I looked at the door as it slowly eased shut on its safety device, and my shaking slowly subsided too.

Months later, when I was told Donna was leaving the college – after knowing that the iron-clad teaching contracts meant she'd never get fired – it was like taking the first breath of air after being released from jail.

It said something about my new found sense of control that I'd made it through Donna without drawing attention to my hatred of her.

A sell out?

Fuck that. You choose the battles you can win and sometimes you win by doing nothing. You win by the freedom it gives you at other times. Saying nothing isn't giving in, lying is. Just last longer than the enemy, as long as you stick to your path when you can.

You win by still interrogating how you think. Realising you fuck up sometimes.

You can't directly win against teachers. The sheer weight of numbers doesn't allow for it. Their political and social views can't be changed... it's hard to even *slightly* modify them.

12

In the spirit of exploration, I tried to see teachers at play. Sure, they often seem overly tetchy, but the job does have its pressures. Catch anyone on a bad day and they can snap.

So I went along to the Christmas party this year. Not because I couldn't avoid the damn event – I'd avoided it for over a decade – but because I wanted to see what the hell happened at them.

It was held in one of the large meeting rooms. No booze, of course. The food was served by the canteen staff, and there were long queues for the two coffee machines set to "free vend."

The atmosphere was odd. Happy and seemingly relaxed, yet slightly stilted and unreal. From the tinsel hung around the staid teaching tables and chairs, to the four carollers (elderly Music teachers) loudly singing out-of-tune Christmas hymns.

The teachers sat almost exclusively according to their subjects, and talked in hushed voices. Lower-level bosses sat with their departments, while the higher bosses sat on a table by themselves. The hum of conversation was flowing easily everywhere. Genuine laughter broke out a few times.

I felt uncomfortable straight away, out of my depth surrounded by so many teachers. I took a bunch of trips to the toilet but I never ran away. I was too scared to draw attention to myself by just disappearing. I was lucky, like some autistic kid, that I'd had years to develop practiced responses to a bunch of stuff I didn't understand or care about.

The conversation on my Media/Film/Communication Studies' table was about the usual things. Unruly students (again). Damn coffee and biscuits (again). And a huge amount of overly positive stuff about their progenies. About how Joshua was great at fucking rugby, or how Anastasia had learnt to speak so fucking quickly, or how fucking Barnaby loved studying at Cambridge.

I kept to my rules, reversing their questions whenever possible:

"So, how is your mother getting on?"

"Well, you know..." I breathe out slowly. "But how's

Barnaby getting on? How's his course going?"

I only cracked once under the barrage of it all. The other Film teacher was talking about her daughter – Anouska – and how she wanted to see a "15" rated movie for the first time.

"She's only 14, but she particularly wants to see *Black Swan*. And..." she leant in to whisper in my ear, "...I was going to smuggle her in because she's so mature for her age. And, as you know, I adore *Aronofsky*." She said his name with real arousal. "But then I discussed it with Harriet and she said there's an explicit lesbian sex scene..."

I acted startled... the right response. But, as I did it, I sickened myself.

She laughed, then looked into my eyes. "Not that it's remotely a problem of course!" She looked to one side. "It's just that wouldn't it be dreadfully awkward watching that together?"

"Well," I said, four slugs of vodka inside me and tired of the whole event, "couldn't you just slide your hand behind her and say: 'Honey, there's something I always meant to tell you?'"

She slapped my arm and rasped: "DON'T BE FILTHY!" and conversation stalled on the table for a minute. I decided to take another whizz.

Walking back, the psychedelic David Lynch mood was being completed by a Maths' teacher who was now reading poems about each teaching department. He was dressed as Santa Claus, and had each of his limericks written on different coloured cards. I don't want to attack the guy, because he was one of the "old school" teachers who were there when I was a student. A lovable eccentric with a wide gut and a sense of optimism.

But the guy wasn't a poet. Fuck, who is? And as he rattled them off, I had to concentrate on trying to smile as the other teachers erupted into self-conscious laughter.

I went to the toilet again straight after the Media/Film limerick and frantically wrote it down....

"There once was a student called Jim,

"Who couldn't concentrate due to a whim,

"He only wanted to watch TV,

"As much as he could see-see,

"So he settled on studying Film."

Yes, I was baffled by the "see-see" too.

Five trips to the toilet, five slugs of vodka and five sticks of gum.

I went back into battle again.

And I behaved beautifully as I looked suspiciously at the three bosses on my table of eight teachers...

13

I'm now 34 and I can count at least sixty people who have a role they consider superior to my teaching post. A standard teacher is almost outnumbered by their bosses. Each sits at the top of the table, or the top of a meeting, or adopts a superior attitude.

First, there's "additional responsibility." On this, you get paid an extra grand for dealing with a lot of extra paperwork. You're second in command to the "Head of Department" (HOD).

HOD is sub-divided into subject groups: English. Media. Maths. Performance Studies etc. You can be Head of Department (£3000-£6000 extra per year) even when you only have one other teacher in your department.

"Senior Tutor." One of those for every ten teachers. Fifteen at my place. They get their own office and deal with troublesome students.

"Head of Curriculum." Six of these... head of department heads. As a Media/Film teacher, my curriculum group is Media/Business/I.T.

"Deputy Principal". You'd think they'd be one of these, but there are three. One science based, one arts based, one humanities based.

Back

All carrots lead towards the role as head-honcho. Principal. £120,000+ a year. No teaching. A personal secretary. It isn't hard to wonder what is required to get that far. Almost all principals are over 50, and haven't taught full-time for more than ten years.

The younger teachers strive to "climb the ladder," while older teachers get very sniffy if they don't get promoted.

The Shane Meadows' obsessed Film teacher – who had the lousiest interaction skills with students – was particularly peeved not to get a Senior Tutor position and still rants about it in meetings. Even though she realises it entails a bunch of paperwork far in excess of monetary reward. The goal is purely to be promoted. *Buy Anouska more stuff. Climb that fucking ladder.*

This leads to a bunch of revolting activities. Firstly, there are "voluntary" tasks. Selling the college at open evenings and education fayres. Secondly – and this is much worse – there are college-based parties. Wilson's son was an adept trumpet player, and Wilson would organise trumpet recitals where teachers could appreciate his son's talent. These would be attended by twenty-plus teachers. All lovers of brass music, I guess.

Climbing the ladder must be a chore. But it becomes second nature.

I think it deflects the focus from putting time into good

lessons.

And how the fuck do you think it makes students feel?

14

I'm now reaching the end of my fifth year after returning to teaching. I still teach half-days... just the right amount of hours. This gives me time to write, act as a carer for my mother, and post books for you lovely Murder Slim Press fans.

I get long holidays but also long periods of marking essays. Yet it certainly beats the shit out of barwork. A good lesson is wonderful... much like a stand-up comedian when the audience laughs at every joke. When a lesson works, you feel a huge surge of happiness. Yes, the job is occasionally frustrating, but it's often damn fun.

I now teach with the now-six-years-girlfriend of my co-editor at Murder Slim Press. She's one of my ex-students, and I get on with her well. My Head of Department is pleasantly respectful and does a great job of leaving me alone. The other Film teacher is an irritant, but I only have meetings with her three or four times a year. In the grand scheme of things, I really can't complain too much.

Yet they'll always be moments that disgust me. I can keep to my rules, but sometimes I need to cut out my tongue.

Every few months, all teachers at college are subject to group training. Motivational speakers come and yap about how to modernise your teaching. How to introduce crossword puzzles into quizzes, or use musical montages to get across key terms.

Or, like today, when one of my sixty or so bosses will guide the teachers on how to improve lessons... despite them seeking promotion largely to take them *out* of teaching lessons.

This latest one is "Equal Opportunities." A noble cause, at least...

15

I make a stupid mistake – breaking a minor rule – by turning up early to the damn event. I head for an empty table, sit in peace for five minutes, before having nine idiot teachers come and sit with me. I find a couple of them particularly objectionable. The backstabbing Dance teacher, and the laddish Music Technology teacher. I should dig a fucking hole and escape. But that will be spotted. Damn...

The Music Tech teacher has a thing for the Dance teacher, so I get a close-up view of his desperate, sycophantic flirting. Whispering in her ear and giggling.

After a one-hour diatribe defining Equal Opportunities and establishing words that are no longer acceptable ("deaf," "blind" and "gay" are amongst these), each table is given a different issue to deal with.

We're given the following:

"You are passing out condom-cards [a genuinely great idea where kids get free condoms] *to your class. As you go to pass out the last card to a female student, a male student shouts out 'DON'T MIND 'ER... SHE'S SAVING IT FOR JESUS."*

Aside from the Dance and Music Tech teachers (still caught in their verbal dry humping) the other teachers on the table are indignant. They want to stop their lesson. They want to lecture the male student. They want to SHOW the rest of the group how wrong his comment was.

I had taken another big swig of vodka beforehand, knowing how objectionable the training would be. And maybe that helped me snap... albeit in a controlled way:

"I wouldn't stop the lesson. I'd have a word with the kid afterwards. You stop the lesson and you make the girl feel like shit. She's the centre of attention. By getting so fucking pissy over the comment, you exaggerate the power of an offhand joke."

I don't win, of course. The two teachers next to me sniff. I'd sworn. I'd said something *unprofessional*. And the rest of the table eventually follow suit.

We then reach the "plenary" stage, where you relate your findings to the room of 150 teachers. Shit, the faces keep changing but their beliefs still don't.

I look around. I'm now one of the last six who are still there from twelve years ago, when I first started. The stupidity remains. It doesn't amplify. It just *is*. Teachers don't learn. *Fuck, that's what I've learned.*

A middle-aged, middle-upper class teacher stands up to give her group's plenary.

"We were given the following dilemma: 'A girl in your class seems to be agitated. A male student shouts out: *'Don't mind her. She's on the blob!'* We were requested to see how we'd deal with the situation."

In a room full of 80% female teachers, I wait.

Charlotte looks around and smiles: "When this sort of event happens, I like to respond with wit, not intelligence."

A few laughs from the room.

"I like to tell the boy that men are full of testosterone. It's *proven* that they think about sex every seven seconds."

A dozen or so teachers applaud. And the vast majority of the rest of the room laughs.

I want to bonk my head on the table.

They'll be another hour of this hypocritical shit to listen to.

A female dominated world as stupid as the male dominated world of the 50s. A world where sexism towards guys is not only fine, but celebrated. Where teachers love the working class, as long as they're kept at a safe distance. Where they claim to celebrate the power of learning, yet practise the dark arts of social climbing.

16

The role of teacher can be like a disease. If you spend too much time around them, you can catch the damn thing. The sarcasm, the gossip, the prissy attitude. I've seen young teachers catch it within two years. Over-elaborate words sink into their conversations and their teaching. *Professionalism* becomes their watchword. Along comes the need for the bigger TV, the bigger car, the bigger house. Acknowledgement from their peers and promotion... career becoming life.

I've come back here. I chose it, but I must keep aware of the situation. I just hope I can keep seeing that, rather than sinking into it. Right now, I can't count any teacher as a close friend.

I'll concede there are probably other free-thinking teachers at college. There's got to be at least one other out of 150. But the effort required to find them is too risky. By sticking to my rules, I'm reticent around all of them and keep my thoughts in check.

I feel contented. I pull in enough money and I get enough free time to do the things I enjoy. Yet my writing consistently veers into rants, where repressed emotions pour out. *Fuck, have I still become like them by bitching about them in this story?*

The role has a weird power, and it infects just as much as it's misused.

It's a word that's revered, because we tend to remember the best of them instead of the grinding majority.

"Teacher."

That word can become your life.

Back

Afterword

It's four years since I wrote BACK and my workplace hasn't changed much. It's a world which seems to slowly multiply rather than deduct its faults. The college – as with all educational institutions – keeps becoming more corporate. I remain a round peg in a square hole... and not in a sexy way.

There is now only one teacher who has been at the same college longer than me, and she'll be retiring next year. Where has the time gone?

I kept BACK stored away because the content will annoy the people I work with if they find it. Yet I increasingly don't care if it ruffles feathers. As long as I last another year, I'll win the longest serving "Ironman" competition. Then I'll quit and become the World's Greatest Skydiver, or something like that.

In 2011, a major publisher was delicately sniffing around my stuff and Murder Slim Press. Seymour Shubin offered to write an introduction to this story, which I had been talking about to both Seymour and Rob McGowan.

Rob was initially critical, and Seymour was insightful. Both were hugely helpful. For that, and for many other reasons, I miss the hell out of both of them and I wanted to say "thanks."

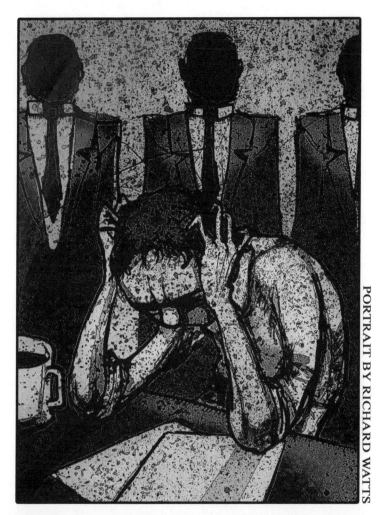

PORTRAIT BY RICHARD WATTS

Steve Hussy worked in shithole bars for years before training to be a teacher. He's now been teaching for 15 years in colleges and universities, predominantly in the North-East of England. He's primarily a Film teacher, but has also taught both English and American Literature.

Hussy helped form Murder Slim Press in 2005, and is currently its main editor. *The Savage Kick* - MSP's literary magazine - has been the launching pad for writers like Mark SaFranko and Tony O'Neill. *The Savage Kick* has also published a number of established writers and artists, including: Dan Fante, Joe R. Lansdale, Jim Goad, Doug Stanhope, Joe Matt, Debbie Drechsler, Steve Rasnic Tem, J.R. Helton, Seymour Shubin, Ivan Brunetti, u.v. ray, and Robert McGowan.

When not busy teaching, editing or doing design work, Steve Hussy likes to write stories. In amongst the booze-driven philosophising, many of them contain rants and scatalogical gags. Ah, let's be honest, all of them do.

STEPS by Steve Hussy

"*Steps* knocked me sideways the first time I read it, and further reads diminished none of its power. To read *Steps* is to see the absurdities at the heart of all relationships revealed under the spotlight's glare."
--- Tony O'Neill, Introduction to *Steps*

"Hussy treads the same broken path [as] Bukowski and Fante... Yet he has a distinct poetic voice, a voice made his own. And the music? A harrowing Waitsian blues."
--- Susan Tomaselli, *Dogmatika*

Chapbook size
62 pages

LONELY NO MORE by Seymour Shubin

Seymour Shubin knows his way around the short story because of the deceptive ease of his prose. But as you're swept into the momentum of any given tale it's easy to overlook all of his other considerable strengths: he's incredibly perceptive, touching, funny, compassionate and versatile, among a host of other qualities."
--- Mark SaFranko, from the Introduction to *Lonely No More*

Sixteen crime and confessional stories
Cover Art by Richard Watts. Lavish interior art
Trade paperback size
128 pages

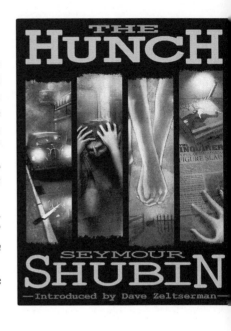
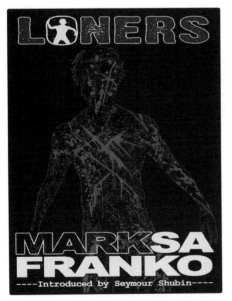

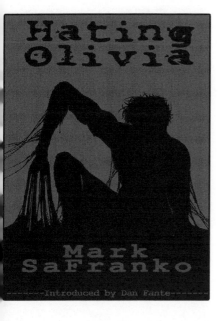
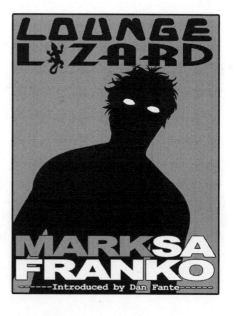

GOD BLESS AMERICA by Mark SaFranko

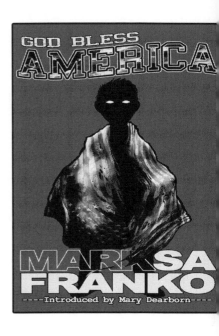

"*God Bless America* is strong stuff. Vomit, blood, piss. Guts. All delivered in scathing, acid prose. SaFranko does not spare the reader in this brutal powerhouse of a novel."
--- Mary Dearborn (author of *The Happiest Man Alive: A Biography of Henry Miller*), Introduction to *God Bless America*

"[It] is not only a passionate character study, it is also beautiful dirty realist fiction in the grand American tradition."
--- Matthew Firth, *Front and Centre*

Trade paperback size
278 pages

www.murderslim.com

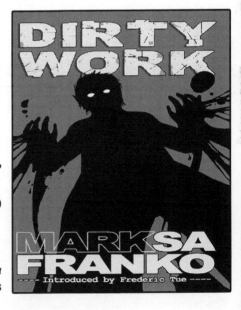

THE ANGEL by Tommy Trantino

"Tommy Trantino has given us the works -
from A to TZZIT. He has put it all in one
book replete with maniacal illustrations as
a handbook to Eternity."
--- Henry Miller

"I haven't read a book in a long time that
has hit me so hard -- a book so fierce, so
poetic, so wise, so heartbreaking."
--- Howard Zinn

In print for the first time in 30 years
Introduced by Tony O'Neill
Chapbook size
92 pages

NAM by Robert McGowan

"[*NAM* approaches its] troubling subject
from all sides, chipping away at the myst-
erious monolith that was the American
war [and] Robert McGowan displays
remarkable range and depth."
---Stewart O'Nan, editor of *The Vietnam
Reader*, a Vietnam War based anthology

"[A] dazzling, harsh, funny and truthful
book."
---*The Veteran*

8 Pages of Interior Art by Steve Hussy
Trade paperback size
218 pages